THE CURSED

POET

THE CURSED

POET

OLIVER FRANCES

The Cursed Poet

Oliver Frances

Edited by: Sheila Steiger

Cover by The Little French eBooks

Published 2024

THE CURSED POET

In memory of Timothy Leary

"It is a miserable state of mind to have few things to desire and many things to fear, and yet this commonly is the case of kings."

Francis Bacon

There are diverse events upon human nature that even the human being has not been able to put under his control. However, humanity has attained, through the centuries, a high level of progress.

An icon of the last century is enormous apparatuses. Wearing a head-mounted display excites the receptor. Such alteration transmits toward the cerebral cortex through a nerve and nerve fibers. The result is the awareness of the occurrence of something by the subject, which might assure existence as the conclusion of the process.

With respect to this case, the head-mounted display (HMD) isolates completely the sight from outside. Each eye focuses its attention upon respective liquid crystal display (LCD), which emits slightly different images so the subject can perceive the whole picture in relief. The subject is immersed in a third-dimension reality occurring in the process unity of the apparatus, and is non-existent in the outer world.

At the time of Eureka!, the entire discovery revolved around humanity. Nonetheless, within the forthcoming century, the invention is regarded as a little step to an ultra-development, which is not chiefly concerned upon science. It includes all the aspects of life; an extraordinary evolution. *When Man declined to worship God for everything that was ruled by His power, man despoiled himself of any inferiority so as to live out his mightiness.*

Although several innovations are of the utmost importance, time has turned them archaic. The dimensions of high-tech apparatus extraordinariness is gauged by the capacity of reproducing the image of a virtual world. Within the projective system, the image is conceded in thought and movement as a real object. Its chief defect is the subject beheld a pre-recorded video, so it cannot handle what is seen, and the emitted image is an area limited by the place where its generator is located. Apart from this, the subject does not have any control over the experience. Somehow, the drawback is overcome by the invention of human robots,

Oliver Frances

which are easily confused with actual human beings. Consequently, the imperfection of the robot is its lack of soul, by which it can be differentiated. The innovation represents a legal issue. Inasmuch as man created a machine with the appearance of the dead, the betrayal of love appears.

These contraptions of the twenty-first century are the furor. Nonetheless, they are not yet capable of commanding man's emotions, neither succumbing death to his whim. Fragility continues reining upon humanity.

There are yet no means to exercise cerebral control, so as to govern the cortical impulses that reach the hypothalamus. From where these emit to the neuro-vegetative system, generating as a consequence, emotional shock arises. Death, with its own vulgarity, recalls man his own vulnerability. In it is engrossed the unimportance of he.

Oliver Frances

Upon the oval-like, pallid face of the bridegroom, tears well up from her limpid blue eyes, conveying an immense sadness. As the thin white candle her slender hands clasp, she weeps inconsolably. The softly gathered skirt tightens to her fragile body, sweeping over the world.

The enormous red dragon, having seven heads, ten horns, and seven crowns upon its heads, slumbering placidly within its den, is awakened. This infuriates the assailed and splendid eagle that traverses the hallowed cope. Whilst the robust and Lyon thunder and threaten to death the Gallus.

The Garden of Eros is the round garden, concealed as a precious treasure inside a den within a remote area of London. Its allure bewilders Psyche, whom is led by ghostly servants to the great hall of the marvelous gilt palace, which is the rendezvous of her Delphic husband. Not christened as Greek mythology, it is named as the Garden of Life, inasmuch as this was not wrecked by the dreadful acid rain. In the center of the garden, the constricted trunk with its thin branches casts out little, ocher leaves, which are tiny flames of life over the unfolded greenish mantle.

The lad is flung upon a bench, as his well-molded features are made to pose by nerve. It appears within the chambers of his brain. Occurring reasoning over art and science is present. A conflict over the whole thing becomes more and more absurd when considering art might well be annihilated in human life. Even though his prepositions and interpretations sought to awaken concepts, in one way or another, they mold the abstractions of humankind. The view is differenced by indefinite ways and the conduction of man in previous centuries.

His discernment is nonplussed by the rare disappearance of a beau. As an ordinary human being, the emotional shock is irretrievable and his brain is not able to exercise any control upon it. Still, within modern era, human nature is beyond any comprehension. Within all his superiority, man is a God of muddied feet. He yet

Oliver Frances

has to rely upon religion, even to attribute to an event of its own origin.

It is a severed garden, with parts suffused by a sun-gilt and tenebrous gloom light. Upon the bright side is where the youth linger, and on the obscure one is the place where the aged behold the days of their lives passed by. He is on the scintillating part, closed in by profuse greenish cascades, which represent sources of life near the flame.

Upon rising his sight, he marvels himself with all the wealth of nature, for which there is no logical reason unmarred by the nuclear war.

Unexpectedly, a rush cascades around the garden, sweeping pages of a prestigious newspaper, which stick to his knees. Once the gust fades away, he clasps the pages and raises them to the height of his view. His eyes focus upon an article entitled, *The Cursed Poet*. The essay is based upon the works, some of them illogical, of a notorious writer of the last century, who depicts in a fantastic narrative a nuclear conflict between the potencies of Earth. At the time, there is supposed to be a long period of

Oliver Frances

international peace, inasmuch as the dismantlement of the diabolic beast erected on the east, whose ambition is to exercise a supreme dominance over the world. Nonetheless, the writer's lucubration turns to be real. Venice, the city where he spent the last days of his doom, is in ruin.

According to a rumor that runs around the city and after the entire world, he, along with his consort, concoct an eerie death by which he never died, as acclaimed. Furthermore, the legend into which the whole affair turned to be is supported by the fact his corpse was not seen within the urn by anyone, except his wife. The journalist concludes, whether the obscure plot about his death is true or not, beyond any doubt, he would at this time be deceased had he remained in Venice or some province of Italy.

It is inconceivable his lines were not to come to pass, and these just to be a *Truth of Blood*. For his rare manuscript had not been senseless before the reality of *The Babylonia of Gaul* erected itself underneath the waters of the Atlantic Ocean. Heaven infuriates throwing

Oliver Frances

brimstone over Earth, as were Sodom and Gomorrah. New York is devastated, and a part of Albion disappears under the Polar waters.

Evidently, the man of the new millennium does not conduct himself in accordance with his conceptualized world. Within several writings of his, as were defined the characteristics of the man of the future, is manifested a being who does not conceive humanity divided by boundaries, nor believe in superiority between ethnic groups. Neither is assented with racism. The cursed poet runs into the ground the immerse vessel representing the whole Darwin theory, which introduced the concepts of *advanced* and *inferior* races. Predominating during the nineteenth-century, a reason to justify the colonial policy of the European countries at the time is developed.

His listless hands place the newspaper aside, upon the bench. Leaping to his feet, he leaves the garden.

Although the awesome article does not excite his attention, at the moment, he cannot avert from it, coming to his reason. It is a rare fact at nights when he is insomniac, the cognomen title granted by the press to the cursed poet suffuses every cell of his brain, arousing an impressive curiosity for such notorious persona. In addition, as life is an illogical fait accompli, by just a mere coincidence or pre-fated event, he runs across a brief biography of the writer on the Internet.

It is the time when Internet exercises dominance over all aspects of human life. This is not the means through which the cursed poet would run the pages of the edition, neither would he squander his precious time as he did in all those places where what was traded was just books. The traditional bookshops closed down a long time ago, by the fierce competence of the great chains and the apparition of digital books.

Just for the record, the affair relates to Mr. Topping's protest where he was the director before. He was dismissed by his reluctance to reduce the stock of the newly published material and for not granting privilege to the best sellers, apart from having as a policy the acquisition of books of little sale with an enormous cultural

Oliver Frances

worth. This was against the commercialization plans of the chains.

Oliver Frances

The account was in bits and bytes. O' Flahertie Oliver, writer, born in Paris (1970 - 2015), under the name Marc Philiphie de Breteuil. The press christened him *The Cursed Poet*, just for the simple fact of writing in English instead of the language of his French ancestors. His works exposed his advanced ideas as he claimed them. They were based upon the unity of the world as one and the dejection of the concept of the *superiority* or *inferiority* of races. Among his writings, stands out the compendium of his thesis about the importance of *Art in Life*. This eccentric existence is a primordial factor for his dazzling creativeness, which his works convey. It is presumed he died in Venice, but presently there is no testimony that confirms this. It is stated the cause of his death as heart failure. Through his writings and the essay, *The Importance of Arts,* the young lad is able to elucidate his own inconsistent theories.

Apart from the social function, which is difficult to gauge, art is the unique means of attaining realization. This might well be evidenced through poets, philosophers, and men

Oliver Frances

of sciences and culture, whom through artistic activities, have found self-expression and realized themselves as identities. It can be presumed as erratic the reference made about men of sciences. However, if it is reasoned through the postulate that by individualism scientists are enabled to develop their own inventions, and as art is individualism, therefore, men of sciences are the most industrious to comprehend art.

Within the third world, art is regarded as a profession for the idle. The man of the South does not concede an important role in their lives, and along with congeners, deprecate those men whom committed their existence to art. The reason for such a conception is due to the lack of a legacy of culture in those lands. Art is at its lowest, for art is culture.

Nevertheless, southern man always has justification for his own conceptualization upon the base that science is the medium to subdue nature and remold society. Its own value lingers upon its vital importance for the world's intelligence, and by which a science man can enrich himself in a disciplined way while liberating his mind. Furthermore, one of science's high aims is to procure a way to give reasoning about the events as a mere truth, and does not support them upon emotions or poetize them to justify their existence. While listening to his exegesis, which is a confrontation against art, the interrogation that comes to mind is why have they not reached a level of development, and what the reason is for which the course of their lives are spent in misery.

The response is obvious. When there is no existence of art, everything is common and vulgar. The work conditions are ordinary and bring as consequence a plain work, because the obscure workman is affected by the mundane workplace. The ordinary human is dependent upon those who have an opinion, created by a legacy of culture and their influences on the environment that surrounds such plain creatures. Therefore, the southern man is ignorant, because he has no mentality. The unbearable burden of the whole tragedy of their lives is that their existence is at the mercy of the cultivated.

This justifies the reason why one country exercises a supreme dominance over another.

Trial of inner logic consistence (conclusion from established postulates).

Scientific----------

Trial of outer logic consistence (conclusion is in harmony within reality).

Laws---------------

To harmonize with other scientific laws.

The scientific value of a conclusion does not depend upon its harmony with reality. It is only derived from the hypothesis already set and is otherwise scientific valueless if it does not comes from the postulates made. Because it is not in accordance with the inner logic, it does not allow scientists to forecast. This is the reason for scientific law.

Science endeavors formulate laws, so as to forecast the forthcoming events. When scientific ideas fail in practice, their inconsistence is entirely. Nevertheless, this fact might add some value to theoretic. The whole field is summed up in one sentence. *Science is not exact and can be at error.*

Consequently, the concept of God runs to ground all science.

Oliver Frances

At noon, the imposing flare of the Astron star lingers upon beautiful Venice. Within the Great Canal, which meanders along and is one of the most splendid of the city with its two domes at both extremes—Saint Simeon Picolo and Madonna de La Salute—the multicolored and painted fresco palaces alter their tones by the light's whim. As the color of a faded rose tints the canal, the architectures turn white, disseminating an incandescent brilliance as though they are divine's dwells.

Through the canals, the polished-wood, long boat is steered. Upon reaching the Great Canal, there is a fine-molded figure of a Venus in black, within whose triste face tearful, greenish eyes covered by veil can be seen. Behind her is an ebony coffin, upon which roses are scattered. Two mortician assistants, whose countenance mirrors sadness in their respective funeral dark attires, escort it.

Rarely, it is regarded that the chief reason for a life is the supreme right to manifest one's own ideas, without granting relevance to the medium.

25

Perhaps, it is as well as the philosopher stated it. *The purpose of life is religious discovery*. For him, the most important and greatest art is life. The cursed poet is the priest of his self-destruction, which seems to end as love comes to his encounter. Nevertheless, as his meteoric career concludes in disgrace and poverty, he, in melancholy, delivers himself up to the nefarious reign. This is the thoughtless use of psychedelic, to free Venus from this tormented existence.

Were one to go through the lives of all artists, it might well be stated that the most abnormal beings are those whom create works of art. The case of a rare conduction is Oliver O' Flahertie's, *The Cursed Poet*, who delivers a great ideal through the concepts of his writings, and whose sort of behavior led him to an alleged death.

From time to time, it is rumored the cursed poet was seen in a European country. Once, a woman stated she lived with him. At the moment she recognized him, which was quite difficult, for she bore in her mind his youthful appearance and not the gray-haired man who put on weight and had ireful eyes and a sad expression, he left her suddenly without traces.

It was Piazza San Marco within all its splendor—the marvelous entrance of the city. Every afternoon, the Venus would stroll around the four places, admiring the majesty of the Palazzo Ducale, which is residence of all magistrates that were between themselves and those who conferred a stable constitution granting the political independence, whilst she mulled upon the concept of who had been her husband in life.

The conception of the writer is based upon the fact of whether the artist's creation is made well or not—it is of no relevance, the importance lingers on the expression. Art holds the man together. What is ad rem was his perseverance and the loyalty to his ideas.

Long before his death, it was revealed to the Venus that his words were not transient and would pass onto future generations. Across her eyes comes a mist of tears, as she lays her sight upon the imposing Byzantine Basilica San Marco consecrated to the saint, whose body in religiosity of the ancient founders represents the legitimation and cause of independence. As she strides at the center of the Piazza, a throng of pigeons arises in flight and she comprehends what the poet's words mean within the verse. *Death makes angels of us all and gives us wings where we had shoulders.* Upon which the cursed poet paraphrases. *It liberates man from his own suffering.*

Oliver Frances

It is a peculiar trait of the English personality to have the seed of *tradition*, which has been sown onto generations perpetually. It is not a rarity to find people that embrace customs from the past, therefore, coming across those places that just trade books. *Bookshops*.

Upon the obscure brilliance of the parquet flooring in the back of the bookshop, which remains as a replica of those of the ancient times, the lad props upon the giant shelf. He ardently reads extracts from the pages of an old cover, which along with the others seems to be vintage, about the biography of the cursed poet.

Some wondrous events of the writer are seared upon the lad's mind, so that at night-time, whilst he slumbers, he will have a panorama of eerie situations, complex arguments, and even dialogues of such a remarkable existence. He is a spectator within that theatre—as his brain is—where on play is the life of a man of letters. There are innumerable conceptualizations about the writings. The one that overwhelms the lad is that upon honesty.

Oliver Frances

A rare conclusion, not based upon logic, has been drawn from his living days. Honesty is the thing sought most, and it is what people despise. The reason can be attributed to the fact that truth is a bitter fruit and it seems better to taste a delicious lie. Perhaps, the human being cannot bear having in his hands what he has dared the world.

Dishonesty is the means through which man carries out his deal satisfactorily. When one plays along with truth in his hands, he is misjudged inasmuch as no one can be upright within a world of scoundrels and traitors. Within his considerations, this is mulled upon by the writer. Fidelity, as self-annihilation. Since faithfulness is the source of frustrations, inasmuch as it is the main factor of depriving oneself of fascinating adventures that draw life out of monotony, it causes the origin of unsatisfied desires.

Upon sexual orientation of man, the cursed poet ponders that heterosexuality is the source of life, for through it derives existence. However, it is not ruled out that man might well have sexual relations with members of his own sex. Even though this is his point of view, he is heterosexual, so his wishes are bound to the female, who is the other half part of his soul. Consequently, his contradictions are a source of strength rather than inconsistency.

Oliver Frances

It is Sunday morning. Ash-colored nebulas drift along London, granting a somber appearance to the city. The lad is over in the other side of the Severed Garden, the lugubrious one. At his side on the wooden bench, is the figure of a man hunched by time, whose strands are grizzled and unkempt. Ruin has turned him into an anonymous person, and its rags are on his genius, which at the time yielded brightness on the blooming days of his maturity. His aqueous orbs, that are the mirror of sorrow, are on the cover of the publication he read athirst. The silence is broken as some words are crossed.

"By the way, I was reading a work of his."

The old man turns around to have the book and raises it before him. "Ironic realities. We live them every day, but none dares to write about. Certainly not. A failure writer would do."

"I have read it…"

The same lad that used to impersonate a writer, but at that time, he was just a failure as artist, wanders through the world with an ironic

33

narrative. Not an impressive one, but with a great deal of context. From it comes his genius.

Oliver Frances

It is a sunny morning. He is at the entrance of the building as two lovely, young ladies slow their pace before a man of rough appearance and wild manners. The lad watches the misses, who are almost in ecstasy by this persona. It is a notorious dreadful combination of his clothes, that remind one of a carnival, and the fact he considers that the world always is in search of what is not the best. Although it is pretended the opposite, the horrible truth is evident when he beholds marvelous creatures who are ignored by the others.

The most advisable is not to be an exquisite persona, and be in rags, so as to reach the most desired. During his adventures, the writer is aware of this fact of life and that he is further away from getting or attaining it.

"Impressive," the lad says.

As he is lost through the streets, he listens to the talking of two men who are indignant about their fate and fortune. The elder curses his own star, owing to fact of having to pay for almost everything in life, even love. The young one covets the other's possessions and does not appreciate his. What is not considered is the sad reality that some men can afford nothing, and do not have the things unappreciated by those who possess them. They are those that do not thank Heaven for the privileges bequeathed upon them. The man that curses his own destiny is not the elected to whom has been disclosed the mysteries of life. Nonetheless, this is not of his fate, he is just a man of his circumstances.

He listens attentively to the old man. "It is not an unusual experience for man to extremely seek what might not come to his encounter, and then later emerges in the horizon when it is no longer needed. It is what the world denominates as *irony*. However, as a theme is within one's reason, there will always be a deluge with snippets linked to it, which might well be labeled as *coincidence*."

The golden card of the poor is prayer. It is used before any proceeding, as though it were a way of affording it. The stranded are those who wish to solve insoluble situations by praying.

Oliver Frances

"Although this is his concept, the cursed poet is completely aware man cannot live without any religion," he says.

Art is the medium through which the veil that conceals the mysteries of life is torn up. Besides, it is the way by which man expresses himself. This is the conclusion that makes the lad.

Oliver Frances

This is the real story that was never related to the world.

Marc Philiphie De Breteuil was born within the West Indies. His parents were descendants of the French, whose family consisted of deceased aristocratic relatives from the French Revolution and a Spaniard immigrant who traveled to America, athirst of opportunities, and settled down within the new continent. He is the fruit of a failed union, by a father who wedded a lady of society for a respected social position, rather than love. After the divorce, Marc and his mother remained in the West Indies, whilst his father returned to the old continent with wealth. Poverty mantled them, so his childhood was precarious, and his school names were not resonant. During those tortuous years, as a way of freeing himself from the torment of such a miserable life, he cultivated the marvelous habit of writing, focusing upon the most fantastic adventures and enriching his appreciation of art.

A life's causality was his rejection from an Art Institution, so he enrolled in a business school.

At the age of twenty, he became a stockbroker. Such an employ would be his until a letter arrived in his hands from a publisher, who praised him for his sonnets, but never granted the opportunity of publishing them. He resolved, with a feverish impulse, to leave everything and lose himself through the life of an artist.

Creation power was a certain demon possessing him, so he yielded to the process of writing manuscripts—mediums to express his own conceptualizations. The writer pre-fated the ancient continent to a place where he would take the world by the storm—which he could not attain. Poverty, once more, laid its oppressive cloak upon him, so he became a mendicant on the London streets. Nonetheless, the aftermath of his failure occurred in America, to where he returned. There is no question that following his studies his great battle became life, which he would fight off on his own.

As time passed by, a new publisher offered to run an edition of his short stories, anonymously. Unexpectedly the material bewildered the critics, so his literary agent had no objection to revealing the author. He did not use his Latin name, so the writer is christened again. This time, conferred to him was the pen name, Oliver O' Flahertie.

His peculiar style of life is not a consequence of his success, just the rare influence a book exercised upon him. Its pages describe a wondrous character, which became the conductor of his life. The same manuscript, which during his adolescence made a sense of panic come over him, ended up alluring him and becoming his counselor.

A mad admiration of beauty is paramount of his trait. In addition, an important characteristic of his personality is his obsessive curiosity.

Music is the most affectionate form of writing, so it is not rare that while listening to wondrous harmonies, he would became unconscious. He concludes one art grants new forces to another.

He considers youth the most appreciated treasure of the world, so he is always among them. It is not unusual that marvelous creatures are in his dwellers at the most luxurious hotels, especially in New York. Such a sort of

Oliver Frances

companion gives arise the strangest rumors about his sexuality. Even though the glorious days of his existence are spent among a throng, at the top there is only solitude.

Similar to a bric-brac shop that sells an assortment of curious objects, his case consists of conferences, lectures, interviews, events, and the media. The merchandise is the variety of personalities he encounters.

The existence of a celebrity became monotonous. Then, the banner of the protest against it became the use of psychedelia. Concerning this, he was also inventive or eccentric, for he elaborated his own substance, which rockets out of his tedious world. The consequence is an alteration of his bodily substance, which impedes him to satisfy the senses of his lovers. Nonetheless, long before, when he was just Marc Philiphie, a voyage of discovery relating to the whole experience acknowledged the hidden virtues of the use of plants and crystals. He can perceive the essentiality of not-self, inasmuch as everything is shown in a different way by perception that is not defined by what is biologically or socially useful. He just beholds from a position his inner and outer world, so that through this medium he can understand himself better.

Oliver Frances

The lad is starting his own religion.
Drop Out-Turn On-Tune In.
Life-Structure-Death.

Oliver's, rather Marc's, fairy stories are based upon a brilliant creativeness and delight the masses who regard them as a sort of anodyne for their lacerated souls, finding in them genuine beauty. The joy of writing becomes an unbearable burden as success is building itself. Like a Babel Tower, where there is no time for creation, nor a desire for it, so he had to slay what he loves.

As decadence succeeds celebrity, the cursed poet becomes the priest of his self-destruction, which is evidenced upon his own humanity. All his fine-molded features of a Greek beauty fade away by the abuse of downers and alcohol. Already, gray strands cover his well-shaped head. His blue eyes no longer portray innocence that mirrors the freshness of a lad, now they are dilated and deviated. His athletic figure is a mass of extra pounds.

Oliver Frances

With his small fortune and wrecked reputation, he resolves to leave the glittering world where he dwelled for so long. He seeks refuge among the islands that were once wild and uninhabited—upon which the people of Veneto formed their villages during their escape from the Gotho.

Within Venice, allured by its beauty, he will spend his last years of life. Nonetheless, before the final chapter of his existence is concluded, he will come across the most gratifying experience, love.

As he is sauntering along Giardinetti Reali, which was planted by Napoleon's order so as to improve his view from the Procurate Nuore, he hears the singing of a woman. Her lovely crooning entrances him. He follows the harmonious tone and finds a young woman of extraordinary beauty. She is overwhelmed, not by his physical attributes, just by the recollection of his exquisite sonnets that his brightness created and made her worship art to the full. The young lady is a priestess of Venus. She has the priceless gift of beauty, which the Gods granted, but snatched away by time. This creature is more marvelous than those of bewildering perfection, whom he haunted with a bouquet of living red-roses and a diamond necklace in his hands, through the corridors of flesh and luxury, love and desire, and above all, exuberance, where Edward VII, Nicolas II, and Guillaume bowed to the most beautiful ladies of Paris.

The verses of his poems allure her to love him madly. Bewildered by her comeliness and the generosity of her soul, he accepts to unite his life to hers. As a supreme form of art, her love returns to him the lust for life, which is conveyed upon the mere joy of living without the imperious necessity of expressing himself in any medium of art. He already expressed himself so long before.

They stroll around the streets, flanked by the peeling façades of the shuttered houses, losing their way inside alleys, until they arrive at the world's oldest ghetto in the most humble and peaceful side of Venice.

Nonetheless, felicity is not due to last long. In the streets of each gustier, the Venus has the vision of seeing his husband, so young as he

Oliver Frances

had been once, with all his Greek fine-molded features restored, and upon the arm of a bridegroom. His pallid face and lifeless blue eyes mirror sadness for the unexpected visitor, carrying him away from her. Upon the revelation, she pursues the intruder. Unfortunately, the foresight fades away.

After a certain time, the cursed poet passes away within rare conditions that are never revealed to the world. **The dream is over.**

Oliver Frances